A science **The Magic School Bus** ®
CHAPTER BOOK
FOOD CHAIN
FRENZY

SCHOLASTIC INC.
New York   Toronto   London   Auckland   Sydney
Mexico City   New Delhi   Hong Kong   Buenos Aires

Written by Anne Capeci.

Illustrations by John Speirs.

Based on *The Magic School Bus* books
written by Joanna Cole and illustrated by Bruce Degen.

The author would like to thank Dan Wharton, Director of the Central Park Zoo, for his expert advice in preparing this manuscript.

ISBN 0-439-56050-0

24 23 22 21 20 19 18 17   09 10 11/0

Designed by Peter Koblish

Printed in the U.S.A.   40

First printing, September 2003

✤INTRODUCTION✤

Hi. My name is Arnold. I am one of the kids in Ms. Frizzle's class.

Maybe you have heard of Ms. Frizzle. (Sometimes we just call her the Friz.) She is a terrific teacher — but she has some strange ways of teaching. One of her favorite subjects is science, and she knows *everything* about it.

The Friz takes us on lots of field trips in the Magic School Bus. Believe me, it's not called *magic* for nothing! We never know what will happen when we get on that bus.

Ms. Frizzle likes to surprise us, but we can usually tell when she's planning a special lesson. We just look at what she's wearing.

Ms. Frizzle came to school wearing this outfit on the day our class was supposed to go to the science museum. I hoped it would be a regular old field trip, but all those plants and animals on her dress made me think the Friz had a wilder adventure in mind. Wild is right. You'll never believe what happened. . . .

CHAPTER 1

"Our trip to the science museum is going to be great!" said Dorothy Ann. (We usually call her D.A. for short.) She stared out the windows of the Magic School Bus. "I can't wait till we get there."

Of course D.A. couldn't wait. She's crazy about everything that has to do with science. I was just glad we were going on a *normal* field trip for once — there was even another class in our grade going. That meant nothing bizarre would happen. I was pretty sure the Friz wouldn't risk making it a magic field trip with Mr. O'Neatly and his class around.

I always want things to go smoothly, but

this time I had a special reason. My cousin Janet was visiting. My parents thought it would be fun for her to spend a day with my class. So far, she'd spent the whole bus ride with her nose in a science encyclopedia.

"I bet the science museum in *my* town is much bigger than the one *your* class is visiting," Janet said without looking up. "*I'm* the best science student in my class."

"Just like D.A. in *our* class!" Keesha piped up.

D.A. was taking a library book from her backpack. She smiled at Janet, but Janet didn't seem to notice.

"I'm sure *I* know more science than *anyone* in your school," Janet said. "My teacher says our class is three chapters ahead of everyone else."

Oh, brother! I didn't care who knew the most science. I just wanted to get to the museum safely! I kept my fingers crossed that nothing out of the ordinary would happen.

"We're glad you're with us, then, Janet. The more brainpower, the better," Carlos said.

"We have to try to beat Mr. O'Neatly's class in the Incredible Edibles Science Challenge."

I explained to Janet that Mr. O'Neatly was the other teacher in our grade. Mr. O'Neatly is not at all like the Friz. His classroom is always tidy, and he never plans surprise field trips. He and Ms. Frizzle are always making challenges to see which class knows more. The last time we had a contest, it was a tie. This time, our class really wanted to win.

"I hope you're all *hungry* to answer questions about the eating habits of animals in the wild," Ms. Frizzle called from the front of the bus. "Mr. O'Neatly will hand out the challenge questions after we get to the museum."

"*If* we get there, that is," said Tim, frowning. "This bus ride is taking forever!"

He sure was right about that. The Magic School Bus had been on the road for what seemed like hours! I couldn't even see the other bus anymore. But I *did* see something that made me worry. Liz, our class lizard, had unfolded a big map. She scratched her head while she turned it this way and that.

"Oh, no. Don't tell me we're lost." I groaned and slumped against the bus seat. "If we don't get to the museum soon, Mr. O'Neatly's class will start the challenge without us. They'll win!"

"*My* teacher never gets lost," Janet said. "Her hair is *much* neater than Ms. Frizzle's. And her clothes aren't as busy."

Uh-oh. I really hoped Janet's know-it-all attitude wouldn't cause trouble during our field trip. I knew Janet liked to brag — a lot. Luckily, no one else seemed to hear her. That's because Janet's voice was drowned out by something louder — the growling in our stomachs!

"Is it lunchtime yet?" said Ralphie. "I'm so hungry I can't think!"

That was how I felt, too. The hollow ache in my stomach made me feel woozy and tired. Even Liz looked hungry. Her tongue hung limply from her mouth. She stared cross-eyed at the map, as if she couldn't see it clearly.

4

"Class, we need to recharge with some food energy — pronto!" Ms. Frizzle said, looking at us in the rearview mirror. "Let's pull into this gas station so we can fuel up the Magic School Bus, too."

From D.A.'s Notebook

All Living Things Need Energy

Energy is what makes things move or change. It's the stuff we need in order to walk, run, think, breathe, eat, grow — and do everything else!

Where do we get energy? From the food we eat!

Food has energy that is stored inside of it.

That was music to our ears! We didn't waste a second taking out our lunch boxes. Soon the bus was filled with the yummy smells of cheese, bread, cold cuts, shrimp salad, bananas, milk, fruit juice . . . you name it!

Looking out the window, I could see Ms. Frizzle talking to the gas station attendant. She was holding Liz's map. I was relieved to know we'd be back on track soon. We might even catch up with Mr. O'Neatly's class before they got to the museum.

When the Friz climbed back on the bus, she looked at all of us eating our packed lunches.

"Variety certainly is the spice of life!" said Ms. Frizzle. "We humans are lucky to be able to get our food from *all* parts of the food chain."

"*I've* been an expert on food chains since kindergarten," Janet said.

Tim looked curiously at the bologna sandwich and apple in his lap. "You mean, this stuff comes from a food chain?" he said. "I thought my mom just got it at the supermarket."

"Sure. But the food you buy in stores comes from plants and animals," D.A. told him. "A food chain shows how animals eat plants and other animals for food." She reached into her backpack and pulled out a library book. "At least, that's what it says in my research."

Like I said, D.A. likes science . . . and research. She opened her book and showed us a page.

"*My* book has a better picture of a food chain than that," Janet said.

"Well, the most important thing to *picture,*" said the Friz, "is that food chains are nature's way of delivering energy to *all* living things."

"That's right," D.A. said. "I read that

7

every living thing has energy. When one living thing eats another, it absorbs some of its energy. So a deer gets energy from grass. And a cougar gets energy from a deer."

A *food chain* is made of a series of living things. It usually starts with a plant, which is eaten by an animal, which is eaten by a *bigger* animal, which can be eaten by an animal that is even bigger still.

Each plant or animal is a link in the food chain.

"Everyone knows that," Janet said.

Uh-oh. Having one science expert in our class was enough for me. Now there were two of them — and they were competing! Why did my parents make me bring Janet? I knew she should have stayed home today. "This could be a *long* field trip," I mumbled.

Carlos took a crunchy bite of apple. "That explains why I get such a *charge* out of eating," he said. "An energy charge, that is."

"Very funny, Carlos," Keesha replied. "But . . . where does your apple gets *its* energy?"

"Excellent question!" said the Friz. "The energy in plants and the energy we get from the food we buy in stores can be traced back through food chains to one source," Ms. Frizzle explained. "It's the source of all energy on Earth."

"A really big refrigerator?" Ralphie guessed.

"No, silly," D.A. said. "It's the sun!"

"I don't get it. How can energy from the sun get into my sandwich?" I asked.

Let There Be Light
by Wanda

The sun is the source of energy for all living things: plants and animals. Heat from the sun keeps our planet warm. Light helps plants make the food energy that all living things depend on to live and grow.

"Take your seats, class." I guess Ms. Frizzle didn't hear me. After she said this, she just sat back down at the wheel and started the engine. She seemed to be in a hurry. Now that our lunch had reenergized us, we could finally catch up to Mr. O'Neatly's class so we could start the Incredible Edibles Science Challenge. I thought we were headed to the science museum.

But you know what? As soon as we started to move, something *very* strange happened.

"I think the Magic School Bus got some

extra energy, too. We're taking off!" Phoebe said.

She didn't mean taking off down the road, either. The front of the bus tipped up — straight up in the air!

We zoomed up into the sky. Carlos squinted into the blinding light that streamed through the bus windows. "This is what I call an *illuminating* field trip," he said. "We're blasting off to the sun!"

❧CHAPTER 2❧❧

The Magic School Bus zoomed upward, past puffy white clouds. Soon the gas station where we had stopped was nothing but a tiny speck far below us.

"Now we'll *never* beat Mr. O'Neatly's class in the Incredible Edibles Science Challenge!" D.A. groaned.

"Not to worry, class. I'm sure Mother Nature can *serve up* the science we need," Ms. Frizzle told us.

As soon as she said that, the whole inside of the bus began to change. Our seats turned into red vinyl booths, with ketchup, salt and pepper shakers, and a menu on every table. A jukebox appeared at the front of the bus.

"The Magic School Bus is a diner!" Tim said. He read the neon sign that glowed above the dashboard. "The Eat 'Em Up Cafe."

"A flying diner?" I said. I looked over at Janet. How was I going to explain this to her?

"What about the science museum?" Janet questioned. "*My* teacher always makes sure field trips go the way they're planned."

Usually, the Friz's far-out field trips make me want to crawl under my bus seat. I would love to go on a normal class trip, just once. But I kind of wished Janet would give Ms. Frizzle and the Magic School Bus more of a chance. At least no one else seemed to be bothered by what Janet said. They were too busy checking out our new decor!

Ralphie picked up a menu — and frowned. "Hey, there's no food on this menu!" he said. "I was hoping for some dessert."

"Really?" I looked at the menu that was on the table in front of me and Janet. Talk about weird. That menu didn't list a single thing to eat. But what it *did* have really surprised me.

13

"It's the Incredible Edibles Science Challenge!" I said.

"The questions we're supposed to answer at the science museum?" D.A. looked at the menu on her table and grinned. "Yes! It looks like we have a chance to beat Mr. O'Neatly's class after all!"

There were six questions on the menu. And they weren't just questions — they were riddles! Janet and I read the first one:

Incredible Edibles Riddle #1

This stuff puts the "green" into green plants. It helps plants trap sunlight and use it to make food energy for all living things. What is it?

Answer:_ _ _ _ _ _ _ _ _ _ _ _

"I'm sure *I'll* find the answer first," Janet said. "My teacher says *my* research books are the best." She opened her science encyclopedia and began reading.

"I had something a little more en*light*-ening in mind," Ms. Frizzle told us. "Class, let's take a ride on a sunbeam!"

She pushed a button, and the Magic School Bus made a screeching turn. The bus got smaller, too. A lot smaller! Soon we were so tiny that we seemed to become a part of the rays of sunshine that were streaming down toward Earth.

"Wa-hoo!" the Friz cried as we streaked along on the bright light. "Class, this lovely sunlight supplies living things with all the energy they need to live and grow."

We all blinked into the white glare. All of us but Janet, that is. She was so busy reading that she didn't look up.

"I still don't understand," Wanda said. "How can we turn sunlight into food?"

"*We* can't," Ms. Frizzle answered. "But our planet is full of glorious green *plants* that can!"

"Wow!" said Tim. He pointed out the bus windows. "Look at all that green!"

Our sunbeam was like a high-speed rocket that zoomed toward a big field surrounded by woods. The grass looked like an endless sea of green. As we got closer, I could see grass and lots and lots of clover. We were so small that each round clover leaf looked like an enormous landing pad.

"Oh, no! We're going to crash-land!" cried Phoebe.

This is the part I really *don't* like about Frizzle field trips. I braced myself, waiting for us to smash into the leaf.

But we didn't crash at all — the bus and our sunbeam struck the clover and went *inside* the leaf.

17

"Who turned on the green lights?" Carlos said.

"The green color is from the clover leaf's chlorophyll!" Ms. Frizzle answered. She pointed at some green clusters that were bunched together inside the clover leaf. "Chlorophyll certainly adds color to a plant's life. It has another job, too — one that's even more important."

Carlos's Q & A

Q. What is chlorophyll?
A. Chlorophyll is a substance that exists only in green plants, marine algae, and special kinds of bacteria.

"This weird green light is making it harder to read about what makes plants green," Janet said. She frowned and held her book closer to her eyes.

"We can do more than read about it — we can see for ourselves!" D.A. said. She pointed to the green clusters outside the bus windows. "That chlorophyll allows plants to trap sunlight and change it into food energy that plants and animals can use."

"Quite right! Animals can't change the sun's energy into food because they don't have any chlorophyll in their bodies," the Friz explained. "But plants have the right stuff."

Keesha's whole face lit up when she heard that. "Then chlorophyll is the answer to the first riddle," she said.

"Bravo, Keesha!" Ms. Frizzle cheered.

Just then, Janet pointed to a spot in her science encyclopedia. "I found it!" she said. "*Chlorophyll* is the answer. It makes plants green and traps the sun's energy."

"Is there an echo in here?" Carlos said.

I couldn't believe it. Janet had been so busy reading that she didn't even realize we had already answered the riddle!

Janet filled in the blank on our menu of Incredible Edibles riddles. "I'm sure *I'll* find more right answers than anyone else," she said. She shot a smug look at D.A., then read the second riddle.

Incredible Edibles Riddle #2

Plants follow this recipe for making food.
Mix together sunlight, chlorophyll, water,
and carbon dioxide gas, and presto!
Carbohydrate food energy is formed. What
is the name of this process?

Answer:_ _ _ _ _ _ _ _ _ _ _ _ _ _

That riddle made me more confused than ever! "Food, food, food," I said. "We keep *hearing* about how plants make food, but I don't see anything to eat."

Ms. Frizzle's eyes sparkled. "Let's take chances! Get messy! And cook up some plant food!"

She opened the bus door, and we all flew right out of the bus! Ms. Frizzle, Carlos, Janet, Ralphie, and Phoebe floated straight toward some water that flowed into the clover leaf from the roots and stems. D.A., Keesha, Tim,

Wanda, and I landed on bubbles of gas that gurgled up through some holes at the bottom of the leaf.

What's for Lunch? Carbohydrates!
by Tim

Most of the food we eat includes carbohydrates. Carbohydrates can store energy – and both plants and animals use carbohydrates to live and grow. All carbohydrates are made of carbon, hydrogen, and oxygen.

It figured that Janet *and* D.A. held on to their books. Somehow, I had hung on to something, too — the menu of our Incredible Edibles riddles.

"*My* teacher never pulls messy surprises," Janet said. She wiped a spot from her book. "How can I research about plants making food with all this guck?"

"It's more than just guck," Wanda said.

"It's water and carbon dioxide gas! Those are the ingredients plants need to make food, remember?"

"*I* know that," Janet said. "I've got all the information right here in my book, after all."

She didn't seem to realize that the information wasn't just in her book. It was all around us! I had a feeling the answer to the next riddle was taking place right in front of our eyes.

We were so small that we had actually landed on top of the tiny particles that made up the water and carbon dioxide gas in the leaf. I grabbed a particle and held on tight.

All the sunshine and chlorophyll around us made everything seem really bright and green. The sun's hot energy made our atoms shake like crazy. The hotter it got, the faster the atoms moved.

"Don't look now, everyone," said Ralphie, "but these molecules are busting apart!"

Ralphie was right. Something was about to happen. I could see how the atoms had come together to make molecules.

From the Desk of Ms. Frizzle

Atoms and Molecules

Every material is made of its own tiny, unique building blocks called *atoms*. When atoms join together, they form *molecules*. For example, when two atoms of hydrogen combine with one atom of oxygen, they form a molecule of water. Atoms and molecules are very small. It takes millions of molecules to make a single drop of water.

Ralphie was sitting on an oxygen atom that was attached to two hydrogen atoms. That was a water molecule. I was on a carbon atom, and it was connected to the two oxygen atoms that Tim and Wanda were grabbing. We made up a molecule of carbon dioxide. But not for long. Things were starting to change.

Pop! The carbon dioxide and water molecules started separating into atoms of carbon, hydrogen, and oxygen that floated inside the leaf — with us hanging on to them! My carbon atom pulled away from Wanda's and Tim's oxygen atoms.

"It's an explosion!" I shouted. Our knuckles were white from holding on. The atoms were moving fast and everyone looked terrified.

Well, almost everyone. Janet was so busy reading that she didn't even see what was happening. I couldn't believe she hadn't fallen off her atom.

Then there was the Friz. She was as cool as a cucumber. "Not to worry, class. It's not an explosion. It's photosynthesis in action!" she told us.

"Photo-WHAT-esis?" Carlos yelled, but we were moving too fast to hear Ms. Frizzle's answer.

Our atoms were swirling around so much that I started to feel dizzy. Then I realized that my hydrogen atom wasn't alone anymore. It was swooping toward other atoms. Before we

24

knew it, almost all of the carbon, oxygen, and hydrogen atoms had joined up in small groups.

"Presto!" said Ms. Frizzle. "We're a glucose molecule. Glucose is a kind of carbohydrate. It's a tasty meal for any plant! It contains the energy the plant uses to live and grow."

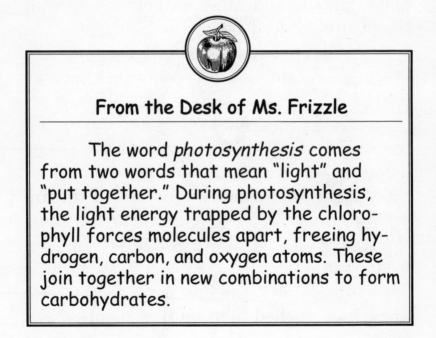

From the Desk of Ms. Frizzle

The word *photosynthesis* comes from two words that mean "light" and "put together." During photosynthesis, the light energy trapped by the chlorophyll forces molecules apart, freeing hydrogen, carbon, and oxygen atoms. These join together in new combinations to form carbohydrates.

I looked around and saw my classmates still clinging to other carbon, oxygen, and hydrogen atoms that were bonding together to make glucose.

Then I noticed there were some oxygen atoms left over. They were floating back out through holes in the leaf.

"So plants are like food factories," said Ralphie. "Thanks to photosynthesis, plants make glucose and other carbohydrates that the plants use for food."

"And the oxygen that's left over goes into the air, where animals and people can breathe it," I said.

"Shhh!" said Janet, without looking up from her book. "How can I read about plants making food if you keep making noise?"

"Actually, I think we just found the answer to the riddle," Phoebe said, giggling. "*Photosynthesis* is like a recipe for making food in plants!"

"Absolutely!" the Friz agreed. "You sure know how to shed light on how plants make food."

Janet finally looked up from her book. "I was just about to get to that part," she said.

We Love Leftovers!
by Arnold

There is always leftover oxygen after photosynthesis. When the water and carbon dioxide molecules combine to make carbohydrates, not all of the oxygen atoms are used. The extra oxygen is released into the air through the plant's leaves. People and animals can then breathe the oxygen.

Janet grabbed the menu of riddles and wrote down the answer. "You're lucky I came along on this field trip, Arnold," she said. "Your class would *never* be able to win the Incredible Edibles Science Challenge without me."

Everyone in my class just stared at Janet. She hadn't noticed a single thing that was going on and she still wanted credit for the answer! But at least we were getting the answers. I hoped Mr. O'Neatly's class wasn't ahead of us, but they had been at the museum for hours by now.

"Hey! There's the bus!" Ralphie said.

He pointed at some new water molecules that were flowing into the clover leaf. Sure enough, there was the Magic School Bus with Liz at the wheel. She steered the bus toward us, and we all climbed on board.

Once we were inside the bus, we sat back down in the booths of the Eat 'Em Up Cafe.

"Ms. Frizzle?" said Phoebe. "Since green plants make their own food, they're at the start of all food chains, right?"

"That makes sense," Wanda added.

"Green plants don't eat other living things, but other living creatures eat *them*."

"You get the picture!" said Ms. Frizzle. "Since animals can't make their own food, lots of animals get the energy they need by eating plants!" She steered the Magic School Bus out onto the top of the clover leaf, and . . .

Bing!

The bus got bigger. We were about as big as a ladybug. As we sat on the leaf, we looked out into the field.

> ## Tons of Plant Food
> ### by Ralphie
>
> Did you know that photosynthesis makes 100 billion tons of glucose and other carbohydrates every year? That weighs more than 600 million blue whales.

"Look at all the rabbits, mice, and grasshoppers in the field!" said D.A. "The rabbits are eating clover. Aren't they cute?"

Cute? I mean, rabbits are okay — but not when they're 50 times as big as I am! Those creatures towered over us like gigantic furry monsters. Every time one came near us, our leaf shook like crazy.

I did some shaking of my own, too — especially when a gray bunny stopped next to us to munch on a blade of grass.

Of course, the Friz was not nervous. Far from it! "Isn't it lovely to *feast* our eyes on the food chain in action?" she said.

We didn't get a chance to answer. Want to know why? As soon as that rabbit finished the blade of grass, it opened its mouth to chomp down on the next closest plant.

Our clover leaf!

"Uh-oh," said Keesha. "We're about to become rabbit food!"

CHAPTER 3

"Noooo!" I shouted.

The last two things I saw before I covered my eyes were the rabbit's huge, razor-sharp front teeth.

Crunch!

I had a sinking feeling in my stomach as I waited to go down the hatch, but . . .

"Phew! Those teeth missed us by a whisker!" I heard Carlos say.

He wasn't kidding, either. When I opened my eyes, I saw that the Magic School Bus had gotten caught on one of the rabbit's whiskers.

If you ask me, we were still way too close

to that chomping mouth. Luckily for us, Ms. Frizzle hit the gas and drove down off the whisker and into the fur. Soon we were perched between the rabbit's ears.

We bounced all over the place as the rabbit hopped around, munching clover. Janet's science encyclopedia almost fell from her lap. It was hard to see out the windows through the rabbit's deep fur.

"Field trips at *my* school never get this hairy," Janet said. "My teacher is neat and organized." Janet's teacher sounded a lot like Mr. O'Neatly.

Whoa! Just then, the bunny started to shake its head. With a jolt, we flew through the air and landed in the middle of the field.

"This field trip is crazy," Janet complained, rolling her eyes. "How are we supposed to learn anything? We just keep flying around."

Usually *I'm* the one who complains about the Friz's wild field trips. But I felt bad that Janet wasn't having a better time. "At least we're finding out about food chains," I said.

"You said it, Arnold!" the Friz called out. "And right now, we happen to be looking at the second link of a food chain."

Phoebe glanced out the bus windows and gasped. There was a grasshopper right next to us, chomping on some clover. "You mean that grasshopper?" she asked.

Which kind of Eater are you?
by Phoebe

In the animal world, there are three different kinds of eaters:
- **Herbivores** eat only plants. (Rabbits, grasshoppers, and deer are a few examples of herbivores.)
- **Carnivores** eat mostly other animals. (Foxes, eagles, snakes, tigers, and many kinds of fish are carnivores.)
- **Omnivores** may eat both plants and animals. (We humans are omnivores. So are bears, mice, and raccoons.)

"Sure," said D.A. "Grasshoppers eat plants, just like rabbits."

"So plants are the food *makers* of the food chain, and animals are the food *eaters*!" said Ralphie. "Insects are part of food chains, too."

"Absolutely! Now we're *really* sinking our teeth into food chain facts," said the Friz.

"Ms. Frizzle?" Wanda said. "What happens to the food energy in grass and clover after a grasshopper swallows them?"

"According to my research," D.A. said, "when an animal eats a plant, it absorbs the glucose and other carbohydrates stored in the plant."

"*My* research gives even more information," Janet spoke up. She pointed at a page in her science encyclopedia. "It says here that the energy an animal eats stays stored inside the animal until it is used for things like growing, looking for food, and running away from other, bigger animals."

"No wonder this grasshopper is chowing down so much. It has to make sure its supply of carbohydrate energy doesn't run out," said Carlos.

"Yes," said Janet.

"Definitely," said D.A.

Janet and D.A. crossed their arms and stared at each other. Let me tell you, there was a ton of energy inside the bus right then. *Competitive* energy between D.A. and Janet, that is.

Eat, Eat, and Eat Some More!
by Arnold

When an animal lives, grows, and breathes, the energy stored in carbohydrates turns into active energy that powers the animal's activities. Once an animal uses up its carbohydrates, it has to eat more food to get a fresh supply of energy.

"Yeah, but . . ." D.A. gazed down at the half-eaten clover leaf that the grasshopper was nibbling. "This insect doesn't absorb *all* the energy from a plant if it doesn't even eat the whole thing, does it?"

"Right you are, D.A.!" said the Friz. "Plants use some of their carbohydrates to live, grow, make food, and reproduce, so an animal never gets all of a plant's energy."

"Plus," Janet said, "my book says that some of the energy gets left behind. It stays in the parts of a plant that aren't eaten."

The rest of us looked back and forth at D.A. and Janet while they rattled off information from their books.

"I guess that's another reason this grasshopper and the rabbit are eating so much," Tim said. "Herbivores have to eat *lots* of plants to get all the energy they need."

"So true!" Ms. Frizzle agreed. "But when animals eat plants, they don't just get energy for themselves. They absorb energy that can become food for *other* animals, too."

"Other animals?" I said. Okay, I'll admit it. When she said that, I was nervous! Can you blame me?

Do the Math (of Food Chains, That Is)
by D.A.

Plant-eating animals have to eat many, many plants in order to grow and stay healthy. That means there need to be a lot more plants than the number of animals that eat them. As you move up the food chain, there are fewer animals at every level.

"Sure," said D.A. "Just take a look behind you, Arnold."

I was almost too afraid to look. I slowly turned around, and I didn't see a grasshopper anymore. I just saw a mouse, and it was cleaning off its whiskers as it chewed on something. I could only guess what had happened to the grasshopper. Still, I was kind of relieved. It was a giant mouse, but it could have been worse.

"So a mouse is the third link in this food chain?" I asked in disbelief.

"You got it, Arnold," the Friz said. "Mice are omnivores. They can eat different kinds of foods, including insects."

I was still thinking about this when I heard Keesha.

"Oh bad, oh bad, oh bad," she said. "I wonder what kinds of animals eat mice."

I didn't like the sound of her voice. I whirled around, and then I saw it. Long and lean and scaly.

"A snake!" I cried.

It was huge. And it was slithering straight toward the mouse — and us!

Its mouth was wide open.

✤CHAPTER 4✤

I wasn't the only one who screamed.

In fact, the Friz was the only one who didn't. She was grinning from ear to ear. "Ah! Here comes the next link in our food chain," she said. She made it sound as if a parade was coming our way, not a snake on the prowl. "Let's take a look, shall we?"

"It might end up being an *inside* look? This is too much!" I said.

The snake struck with lightning speed. Luckily for us, Ms. Frizzle was even faster. She hit the gas, and the Magic School Bus made a flying leap away from the mouse. We landed safely on a blade of grass.

Too bad the mouse wasn't as lucky. It disappeared into the snake's enormous mouth.

"Eeeeew!" Wanda said.

"Class, that snake is the fourth link in this food chain," Ms. Frizzle explained. "Clover, grasshopper, mouse, snake."

"That's not the end of the food chain, either," D.A. told us. She pointed at a page in her book. "The snake could be eaten by another animal, which could be hunted by *another* one. Some food chains have five or six links in them — or even more. And energy is passed from one link to the next along the way."

"Wow," said Carlos. "So food chains really *are* a way to deliver the sun's energy to all living things."

"When the sun shines in, it powers life on the whole planet," Ms. Frizzle agreed.

"Including the fiercest animal hunters, like bears and hawks," D.A. added. "Those animals are at the top of the food chain, so they're the last creatures in the chain to get the carbohydrate energy that plants make."

"*I* know all that already," Janet said. She held up the menu of Incredible Edibles riddles. "Shouldn't we answer the next riddle?"

Incredible Edibles Riddle #3

One single food chain can't tell the whole food story of an area, but this can. It is made of many food chains that overlap and are connected. What is it?

Answer: _ _ _ _ _ _ _

"Huh?" Phoebe said. "How can food chains connect?"

"*I'll* get the answer," Janet said. She tapped her science encyclopedia. "I'm sure it's right here in my book."

"Books are a great way to learn," Ms. Frizzle agreed. "But there are *other* places to find answers, too." The Friz's eyes twinkled like stars when she said that. The next thing we knew, the Magic School Bus started changing again. We still looked like the Eat 'Em Up Cafe on the inside. But the outside of the bus got a lot longer. And scalier.

"We're a snake!" said Keesha.

After seeing what the real snake had done to the mouse, I wasn't crazy about the bus turning into one. But no one else seemed to mind.

Ms. Frizzle hit the gas, and we slithered through the grass toward the woods. Talk about wildlife — there were animals everywhere in that forest! We saw insects, mice, snakes, squirrels, birds, deer, foxes . . . even a bear!

I was glad when the Friz steered the Magic School Snake beneath a big, flat rock. We were almost totally protected. Only the very tip of our tail stuck out.

"Class, the animals in this forest ecosystem live together in a wonderful balance," Ms. Frizzle explained.

"You call this wonderful?" said Carlos. "It's a total feeding frenzy!"

What Is an Ecosystem?
by Ralphie

An ecosystem is a community of living and nonliving things. Every ecosystem is different. A pond ecosystem might have soil, water, algae, insects, frogs, and fish. A desert ecosystem might have sand, scorpions, and cacti.

Frenzy was right. Deer, squirrels, and grasshoppers were eating grass and other plants. Woodpeckers, frogs, and skunks were catching insects like crazy. Foxes, raccoons, and snakes were chasing mice and frogs. A huge brown bear was splashing out of a stream with a fish in its paws.

"Wait a minute," said Tim. He pointed to some worms that were diving into the earth near our rock. "Food chains show each animal eating just one kind of animal or plant. But I see birds and a raccoon eating those worms."

45

"And look at those snakes." Keesha pointed to a snake that slithered toward a frog at the edge of a pond. A second snake was nearby, hungrily eyeing a small rat. "They're hunting different kinds of animals."

"Most animals are like people — they like more than just one kind of food," Ms. Frizzle told us. "That's why lots and lots of different food chains can exist in an ecosystem."

Ecosystems Can Be Big or Small
by Tim

An ecosystem can be as small as a pond or a cave, or as large as a forest or an ocean. When an ecosystem is big, more kinds of animals live there. Food chains in a big ecosystem usually have more animals in them than food chains in a smaller ecosystem.

Janet glanced up briefly from her book. "Listen to this! It says here that food chains overlap. A single animal might eat lots of different animals or plants," she told us. "And get *eaten* by different animals."

Oh, brother. Janet was doing it again. She was so caught up in her reading that she hadn't noticed what the rest of us were watching outside.

"I *see* what you're talking about," Ms. Frizzle said, nodding out the window. "That's why a food chain doesn't tell the whole story."

"But a *food web* does!" announced D.A. "I think that's the answer to the third riddle. It says it right here in Janet's book."

I looked over, and I could tell D.A. had been reading the science book over Janet's shoulder.

Janet stared at D.A. "That's not fair. I'm the one who found the page," Janet complained.

"I know," D.A. replied. "But when I saw *food web,* I thought it might solve our riddle. I'm sorry, Janet."

I believed that D.A. was sorry. I don't think she meant to take away Janet's answer, but Janet wasn't ready to forgive her.

Phoebe's Food Quiz

Q. What kind of web is made of chains?

A. A food web! A food web is a network of overlapping food chains that shows the different eating relationships between animals in an ecosystem.

Ralphie grinned from beneath his base-ball cap. "D.A.'s right. We have the third answer."

Food web fit perfectly when I wrote it down on our menu of Incredible Edibles rid-dles. At least, I *tried* to write the answer. Be-fore I could, Janet took the menu from me.

"The answer to this riddle is *food web*," she said, grabbing my pencil, too. "I was the one who found it here in my book." She wrote it down, then looked triumphantly at D.A. "I just didn't yell it out."

D.A. didn't say anything. Not to Janet, anyway. But she did whisper something to me. "You know, Arnold, if Janet bragged a little less, she might see more of what's going on."

You know what? I was starting to wish this field trip would end. I didn't like being caught in the middle. "Let's read the next rid-dle, okay?" I said.

Janet looked like she wanted to say some-thing else to D.A., but instead she looked down at the menu. I peeked over her shoulder to read the riddle, too.

These omnivores are among the top animal hunters in the world. Sometimes they eat food from food chains in nature. Sometimes they control their own food chains to make sure they have the food they want and need. What are they?

Answer: _ _ _ _ _   _ _ _ _ _ _

"That riddle makes it sound like we're looking for something at the top of a food chain, right?" Tim said. "You know, something like a bear or wolf or eagle. A good hunter."

"I don't like the sound of that," I said. I didn't want to think about top hunters, even as the answer to a riddle. "Top hunters like bears can be fierce," Ms. Frizzle admitted. "But there aren't very many top predators in the wild — not nearly as many as animals that are lower down on the food chain."

"Why not?" Carlos wanted to know.

"It's all about energy, class," Ms. Frizzle told us. "Animals need energy, but there is less energy available toward the top of the food chain."

"In my book, it is pictured like a pyramid," D.A. explained. "The bottom level, which is the biggest one, has tons of plants. Then come the herbivores — there aren't quite as

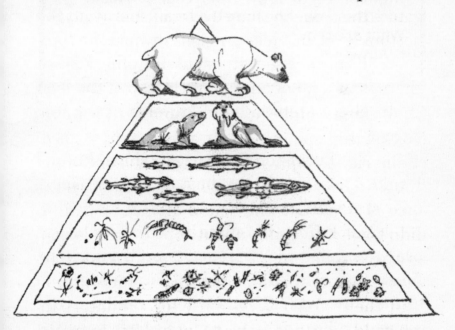

many of those. There are even fewer animals on the next level, and the level after that. Once you get to the level with the top predators, there aren't very many animals at all."

"What does that have to do with energy?" Ralphie asked.

"Well, the sun's energy is passed up the pyramid when one level becomes food for the next. But the animals and plants and insects in each level use some of the energy before it gets passed on. So there's a lot of energy on the bottom level, but less and less toward the top."

"I think I get it," said Ralphie. "Since there isn't a lot of energy at the top of the food chain, there aren't a lot of animals at the top, either!"

Was I ever relieved to hear that! "Phew!" I said, looking out the bus windows. "Not a bear or a wolf in sight."

But I *did* see something else — a bright orange salamander that scampered across the forest floor. The Magic School Snake began to slither toward it. That's when I realized that we were a hunter, too. I couldn't bear to watch as we got closer to the little lizard. I could see the bus-snake's long tongue slide in and out of its mouth. Just as I thought it was going to strike, a piercing screech echoed through the air.

Long-Lost Energy
by D.A.

Plants and animals use most of their energy to live and grow. When an animal eats a plant, it only absorbs some of the plant's energy because the plant has already used the rest. The same thing happens when a carnivore eats another animal.

An herbivore needs to eat a lot of plants to get enough energy, so there need to be more plants than herbivores. And there need to be more herbivores than carnivores.

Janet frowned. "*My* teacher never lets loud noises interrupt our work," she said. "I can't read with all that squawking."

Tim looked out the windows — and

gulped. "Um, Ms. Frizzle?" he asked. "Are *hawks* top hunters?"

Ms. Frizzle nodded. "Hawks, eagles, and owls are some of the fiercest hunters on the planet," she answered.

At that moment, the bus-snake was yanked from the forest floor. We had to grab our seats to keep from falling to the back of the Eat 'Em Up Cafe.

I looked out the window and saw the hawk. It had huge, flapping wings and the pointiest, deadliest beak I had ever seen. The hawk's sharp claws clutched tightly around the Magic School Snake, right behind its head.

"Oh, great," I groaned. "One of those fierce hunters just nabbed *us!*" I looked down at the ground and saw the little salamander run away.

✤CHAPTER 5✤✦

The hawk flew higher and higher, with the Magic School Snake swinging from its claws.

"*My* teacher would never leave our class dangling," Janet said. She buried her nose deeper in her book. "But I won't let that stop me from getting the answer to the riddle."

"Who can worry about riddles at a time like this?!" I yelled.

Trust me, I did *not* want to think about what would happen if the hawk let go of us. I didn't want to think about what would happen if it *didn't* let go of us, either!

"I never knew that we could learn about

55

the food chain just by *hanging* around," Carlos said.

"Being a captive audience *does* have some advantages," said the Friz. "Class, look down there. We have a bird's-eye view of another kind of food chain. It's a food chain that *people* control."

"Huh?" Ralphie glanced down at the ground. "All I see is a bunch of cows and some barns," he said.

Somehow, I made myself look, too. The hawk had carried us away from the woods. Now there were farms beneath us. Cows grazed in a pasture near some cornfields. Pigs, chickens, and other animals ate from troughs next to some barns.

"I think I know what you mean," D.A. said. "When farmers grow crops or raise animals like cows and chickens, they take control of a food chain that supplies people with food."

"Precisely!" Ms. Frizzle agreed.

Janet turned a page of her encyclopedia. She didn't seem to hear anything the rest of the class was saying.

"So corn and other crops are the first link in a farming food chain," Keesha said. She looked out the windows at the green leafy tops of cornstalks below. "They take light energy from the sun and turn it into carbohydrate energy that other animals use for food."

"Definitely," D.A. told her. "Cows, pigs, chickens, and other farm animals are the second link in the food chain because they eat corn and other plants that farmers grow."

"You're so right!" said the Friz. "There's

one more level in this food chain, too. Can anyone tell me who is at the top?"

"People are!" Tim said.

"They sure are," Ms. Frizzle agreed. "Tim, you're really *digesting* the facts on food chains."

"Not as fast as *I'm* digesting the facts in my book," Janet bragged. "My information says that people eat more than just meat."

"Of course," D.A. agreed. "We eat lettuce, corn, wheat, soybeans, all kinds of fruit, and lots of other plants, too. People who are vege-tarians don't eat any meat at all."

"That's right. Humans can eat both plants and meat. That makes us omnivores!" said Phoebe. She smiled and held up her menu of riddles. "So *we're* the top predators that eat food from nature and from food chains that we control. The answer to the fourth riddle is *human beings!*"

"Way to go, Phoebe!" Tim said, giving her a high five. "Just two more riddles to go!"

Janet sat up straighter. "Thanks to *my* research," she said.

I wasn't sure which was worse — being trapped in the claws of a hungry hawk or having to listen to Janet's bragging.

"Is energy lost in a human-controlled food chain, too?" Phoebe asked.

Janet opened her mouth to answer, but D.A. beat her to it. "Energy is lost between the links of every food chain," D.A. said.

Hearing that made me think about something. "If there are so many plants at the bottom of the energy pyramid," I said, "wouldn't it make more sense for *all* animals to eat just plants?"

"Every ecosystem has a balance that depends on animals eating different things," Ms. Frizzle explained. "If all animals ate plants, then when the animals reproduced there would be too many of them. They would eat all the plants until there weren't any left."

"And if plants died out, then animals would die out, too," D.A. said. "But if some animals are herbivores and other animals are omnivores and carnivores —"

"Then there's enough food for *all* the

creatures in an ecosystem to survive," Janet spoke up before D.A. could finish.

I just hoped I would survive the competition between D.A. and Janet. Not to mention our ride in that hawk's clutches!

"We're coming in for a landing, guys!" Wanda announced.

Plant Food vs. Animal Food
by Arnold

An area of land will always be able to feed more herbivores than carnivores. Here are some farming facts to explain it:

If a farmer has 1 1/2 acres of corn, he could use the corn to feed 10 people.

BUT if the farmer feeds that corn to cows and uses the cows for food, the corn will feed just 1 person. That's because energy is lost between levels of the food chain.

The hawk landed on a tree at the edge of a salt marsh. The other side of the marsh opened out into the wide ocean beyond.

But we weren't interested in looking at the view of the water — not while the hawk kept its claws tightly wrapped around the Magic School Snake.

"I do *not* like the hungry gleam in those beady eyes," Keesha said. "And look at its beak!"

"Do I have to?" I mumbled.

All of a sudden, the hawk made its move. Its head darted toward the Magic School Snake — and *us*!

"Yikes!" I cried, shrinking back against my seat. "We're dead meat!"

✤CHAPTER 6✤✤

I couldn't watch. It was too awful.

"Not to worry, class," Ms. Frizzle told us. "The Magic School Bus has what it takes to *wriggle* out of a tight situation."

She pressed a button on the dashboard. The Magic School Snake began to thrash and twist like crazy. It felt like we were on a bucking bronco!

"Oh, no . . . my book!" Janet cried.

Her science encyclopedia flew from her hands. The jerking movements of the bus-snake made D.A.'s book slide off the table of her diner booth.

"There goes *my* book, too!" said D.A.

We were thrashing around so wildly, we couldn't see where those books went. But you know what? The bus-snake's sudden movements did the trick. The Magic School Snake twisted free of the hawk's claws. As we dropped through the air, we saw marsh grass and cattails.

Splash!

We landed right in the salt marsh. Water bubbled up quickly around the bus windows. I looked over to check on Janet, but she hadn't even noticed. She was too busy looking under our booth for her book. D.A. was searching behind the jukebox.

"That's weird. I don't see our books anywhere," D.A. said. "It's almost like the Eat 'Em Up Cafe *really* ate 'em up!"

"Well, it wouldn't be the strangest thing that ever happened on a Friz field trip," Ralphie said.

Janet did *not* look happy to hear that. "But . . . how can I learn about food chains without my research?" she said. "Now we'll never be able to answer the last two Incredible Edibles riddles!"

"Don't be so sure," Tim said. "The Friz's field trips can turn up some surprising information. Just look around!"

"Huh?" Janet was still on her hands and knees. She didn't look out the windows, but the rest of us did. That was when we noticed that the Magic School Bus had changed *again*. Instead of a long, scaly snake's body, we now had gills, fins, and a tail that waved gently in the water.

"We're a fish!" said D.A.

"Swimming with fishes is a great way to see the small creatures that are at the bottom of a marine food chain," Ms. Frizzle told us.

"Like those periwinkles!" Keesha pointed to a large cluster of tiny sea snails that had attached themselves to the marsh grass. "They're eating the marsh grass that's growing on the bottom of the marsh floor, right?"

"You bet, Keesha!" Ms. Frizzle agreed. "A food chain in the water works just like one on land. The carbohydrate energy in the marsh grass gets passed along to the periwinkles. And some of that energy gets passed along to the next link in the food chain — the animals that hunt periwinkles for food."

"That makes sense," said Carlos. "Except . . ." He bit his lip and glanced around. "Where *are* the animals that eat periwinkles?"

We looked around. We didn't see any creatures hunting periwinkles in that marsh, but not all of us were looking at the periwinkles.

"I'm sure *I* can find the answer — if I can find my book, that is," Janet said. She kept looking behind our seats, on the floor beneath the booths — everywhere *except* out the windows.

Finally, Ralphie pointed to a blue crab that scuttled up a stem of sea grass. It grabbed a periwinkle in its snapping claws. "Well, there's one predator," Ralphie said. "But there are hundreds of periwinkles. Why aren't more crabs eating them?"

Wanda pointed to a boxlike wire trap that was half hidden behind the stems of marsh grass. "Because they're stuck in there!" she said. "There must be half a dozen crabs in that trap!"

As the Magic School Fish swam around the marsh, we saw other traps, too. Four of them! They were all filled with crabs that couldn't get out.

"Sometimes things happen to upset the balance that exists between living creatures in an ecosystem," Ms. Frizzle told us.

D.A. nodded at the wire traps. "Like

when fishermen catch too many crabs?" she said.

"Precisely! Without more crabs eating periwinkles, the periwinkle population is growing out of control," the Friz explained. "There are so many of them that they're starting to destroy the marsh grass they use for food."

She sure was right about that. I saw that there were areas where there wasn't any grass at the bottom of the marsh. I could see just a few blades of grass sticking out of the mud.

"Yuck," I said. "Without the marsh grass, this place will be nothing but mud."

Keesha frowned. "Then there won't be any food for the periwinkles, and *they'll* die out, too," she said.

"It's the sad truth," said Ms. Frizzle. "A change in one link in a food chain can affect *all* of the animals in the chain. The whole ecosystem can change. That's why we need to do our part in taking care of Earth."

"I'd say big changes are happening right now," Carlos said. "We're heading right out to sea!"

Did I really need to hear that? No way! But when I looked out the bus window, I saw that Carlos was right. "Come on, kids," Ms. Frizzle said. "If we're going to tackle those riddles, we need to do some deep-sea exploration."

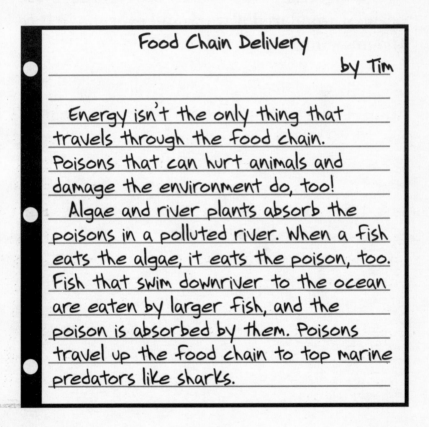

Food Chain Delivery
by Tim

Energy isn't the only thing that travels through the food chain. Poisons that can hurt animals and damage the environment do, too!

Algae and river plants absorb the poisons in a polluted river. When a fish eats the algae, it eats the poison, too. Fish that swim downriver to the ocean are eaten by larger fish, and the poison is absorbed by them. Poisons travel up the food chain to top marine predators like sharks.

I heard the motor start, and Ms. Frizzle steered the Magic School Fish away from the marsh. The Friz was humming "Row, Row, Row Your Boat." Before long I couldn't see the shore or the marsh anymore. All I saw in every direction was ocean, ocean, and more ocean. I wondered if we would ever make it to the museum.

❧CHAPTER 7❧❧

I looked up at the sunlight that filtered through the ocean water. "Wow. We're really in deep now," I said.

"*I'll* say. I'm in deep trouble without my book," Janet huffed. She stopped searching the bus and flopped down next to me in the booth. "Too bad *your* teacher isn't as organized and neat as *mine,* Arnold."

"Actually, Arnold was talking about being deep in the ocean ecosystem," D.A. said. "Take a look!"

Even I had to admit it was pretty amazing. There were sea creatures all over the place! We saw tiny shrimp and lots of fish swimming in schools — little herring, bigger fish like sea bass and mackerel, even some huge sharks. We couldn't stop watching.

Well, most of us, anyway.

"In *my* class, we don't stare out windows when there's work to do," Janet said. "Shouldn't we be answering the Incredible Edibles riddles?" Janet took the menu from my hands and started to read.

But you know what? I saw Janet's eyes stray to the windows of the Magic School Fish, too. Now that she didn't have her book, I guess she couldn't help it.

"Well, the next riddle *is* about oceans," she said.

Incredible Edibles Riddle #5

They are the first link in most ocean food chains. They have the same job as green plants on land — they make carbohydrate energy. They may be small, but they do big work. What are they?

Answer: _ _ _ _ _ _ _ _ _ _ _ _ _

Just then, a shark appeared outside the bus windows. Janet's eyes got huge when she saw the shark dart toward a school of tuna. It grabbed a tuna in its jaws and bit right through it.

"Wow! This is even more realistic than the photos in my book," she said.

We all smiled. Janet was finally getting the picture!

"Sharks are at the top of the food chain, right?" Phoebe said. "But to answer the riddle, we need to find the food-making creatures at the *bottom* of the chain. So we need to find something smaller."

Janet was still staring out the windows. "Hmm. Those little shrimp are eating something," she said. "Their food just looks like specks of dust in the water."

"Excellent observation, Janet!" said Ms. Frizzle. "Those little shrimp are called *krill*. And the specks you see are actually plankton and phytoplankton that krill and other ocean animals use for food."

Floating Fish Food
by Ralphie

Plankton are very small plants and animals that float in seas and lakes. Lots of plankton contain chlorophyll. They are called phytoplankton. (The word phyto means "plant.") Billions and billions of phytoplankton use sunlight to make carbohydrate food energy.

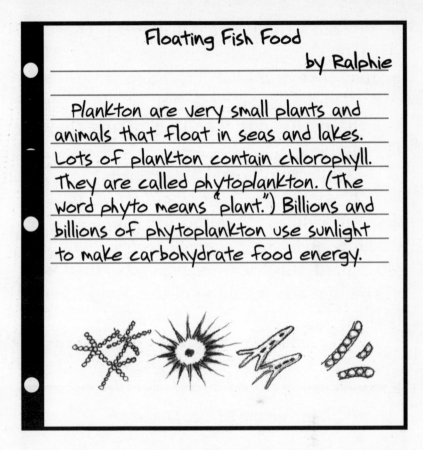

"That's a lot of fish food!" Janet said. She kept staring at the phytoplankton.

"You said it!" the Friz agreed. "Phytoplankton are responsible for 75 percent of the photosynthesis that takes place on our planet."

"That's a big job," I said.

"That's right, Arnold!" Wanda looked at our latest Incredible Edibles riddle. "That means *phytoplankton* is the answer!" she said. "They are the first link of most ocean food chains. Even though they're tiny, they do big work!"

"Quite right!" said Ms. Frizzle.

I wrote down *phytoplankton* on our menu of riddles. I waited for Janet to start bragging about how *she* was the one who was getting all the answers. But she just kept looking out the windows of the Magic School Fish.

"Just one more riddle to go!" I said.

Incredible Edibles Riddle #6

They like leftovers! They break down dead plants and animals into simpler materials that living plants use to make more carbohydrate food energy. They are fungi, bacteria, worms, and insects. What is another name for them?

Answer: _ _ _ _ _ _ _ _ _ _ _ _

While we read the riddle, the rumbling of our engine suddenly stopped. "Hmm. Looks like there's seaweed caught in our propeller," Ms. Frizzle said. "I'll just go out and untangle it."

The next thing we knew, our teacher was swimming outside the Magic School Fish in her scuba gear.

"The buses at *my* school never get seaweed caught in the propeller," Janet said.

I groaned. But D.A. leaned over and said to me, "At least now she's paying attention."

"I think we should *all* be paying attention," Carlos said suddenly. "To that shark!"

He pointed out the window — toward a mouthful of razor-sharp teeth. It took me a second to realize that those teeth belonged to a huge shark.

And it was swimming straight toward Ms. Frizzle!

✤CHAPTER 8✤✤

"Ms. Frizzle, look out!" we all shouted.

The Friz didn't see the shark. She was yanking on some seaweed that was wrapped around one of the propeller blades. With one big yank, she suddenly pulled it free. I heard the motor sputter back to life, and the bus-fish shot forward in the water. We darted away from the shark in the nick of time, with the Friz hanging on to our fin.

"Wa-hoo!" her voice came through the jukebox.

A split second later, the shark caught a sea bass with a giant chomp of its teeth.

"Yuck!" Phoebe grimaced as the sea

bass's fin and some bits of uneaten meat floated in the water around us.

Janet and D.A. were both glued to the windows.

"Class," Ms. Frizzle said through the jukebox speaker, "we have just one riddle left. And here's our chance to see exactly how uneaten animal food gets recycled." When we looked outside, we saw her pointing at the fish fin that fell slowly through the ocean water. "Follow that fin!"

Liz was already at the wheel. She followed the fin deeper and deeper, with Ms. Frizzle holding on to the outside of the busfish. We didn't stop until the fish fin dropped onto the ocean floor.

Tim made a face when he saw all the dead sea animals scattered around the sea bass fin. "That stuff is just lying there," he said. "I don't see anything breaking it down into simpler materials, like it says in the riddle."

Janet pressed her nose against the window. "The riddle answer has to be out there. Too bad we can't get a closer look," she said.

Ms. Frizzle was back, and she smiled at Janet. "Oh, but we can!" said the Friz. She pulled a lever, and a big microscope swung up over our windshield.

"Whoa!" Keesha said. "That fish fin looks huge now!"

The microscope made the fin look a thousand times bigger. Now I saw lots of other things, too. Little spirals, balls, and rods covered the surface of the fin.

"What *are* those things?" I asked.

"Class, those are bacteria. They are tiny living things that are too small to be seen with the naked eye. They feed on dead animals and plants," Ms. Frizzle explained.

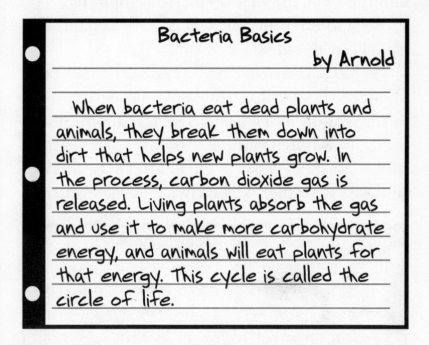

Bacteria Basics
by Arnold

When bacteria eat dead plants and animals, they break them down into dirt that helps new plants grow. In the process, carbon dioxide gas is released. Living plants absorb the gas and use it to make more carbohydrate energy, and animals will eat plants for that energy. This cycle is called the circle of life.

"Bacteria aren't the only things that break down dead plants and animals," D.A. pointed out. "Fungi and worms do the same thing."

"So do little insects like ants and beetles," Janet added. "I read about that in my encyclopedia — before it disappeared. I think there's a special name for living things that break down dead plants and animals. . . ." She snapped her fingers, trying to remember.

"I read that, too," D.A. said, biting her lip. "They're called . . ."

"DECOMPOSERS!" D.A. and Janet both shouted the word at the exact same time.

Wanda looked down at our menu of Incredible Edibles riddles.

"Hey! Good work, guys! That's the answer to the last riddle!" she crowed. "*Decomposers!*"

A Word from Arnold

The word *decompose* means to break things down into simpler substances.

Decomposers such as bacteria, fungi, and worms help to recycle carbon dioxide into the air — and nutrients into the soil — so that plants can use them to make more carbohydrates.

"Yes!" I said. "We did it! We answered all the Incredible Edibles riddles — without even going to the museum!"

You know what was even better? D.A. and Janet were actually smiling at each other. They gave each other a high five while Wanda wrote down the answer.

"Plus, we managed not to get eaten by a rabbit, a snake, a hawk, or a shark!" Phoebe added.

We looked out the windows of the Magic School Fish. There wasn't a thing in front of us except a cloud of tiny krill. What a relief!

"We might just get through this field trip in one piece after all," I said.

"Oh, yeah? Look again, Arnold," said Janet. She pointed behind us.

That was when I noticed the whale.

✦CHAPTER 9✦

The whale was so huge that it seemed to fill up the whole ocean! It swam toward us. As it got closer, it opened its mouth.

"We've got to swim away!" Ralphie yelled. "Quick!"

But not even the Friz was fast enough this time. Before we knew it, the Magic School Fish was swept right inside the whale's huge mouth.

"Oh, no!" I cried. "We've been swallowed by the biggest predator of all!"

"Baleen whales may be big," said Ms. Frizzle, "but they're also the gentlest carnivores in the sea."

We looked out at the tiny shrimp that swam alongside us inside the whale's mouth. There were millions of them!

"So, baleen whales get *high* marks for size," said Carlos. "But they're still *low* on the food chain."

"That's great," I said. "As long we aren't part of *that* food chain!"

But it didn't look like we could do much about it. The whale's mouth was closing! All the water was rushing out, and all the krill were getting caught in what looked like a giant curtain at the top of the whale's mouth.

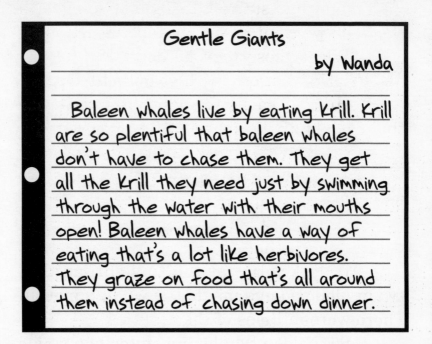

Gentle Giants
by Wanda

Baleen whales live by eating krill. Krill are so plentiful that baleen whales don't have to chase them. They get all the krill they need just by swimming through the water with their mouths open! Baleen whales have a way of eating that's a lot like herbivores. They graze on food that's all around them instead of chasing down dinner.

"That curtain is made of baleen," Ms. Frizzle explained. "It filters out the krill so the whale can swallow it."

"What about us? We're trapped, too! We'll be swallowed!" Phoebe said.

"Not necessarily," Ms. Frizzle told us. "I think we've learned what we can here."

She pushed a button on the dashboard. The next thing we knew, the Magic School

Fish motor had started. Instead of going with the krill, we went in the opposite direction.

"While those krill go down the hatch," Ms. Frizzle went on, "we'll go out, out, out!"

"Huh?" I said. I couldn't believe it was that easy, but with a rev of the engine we were out of the whale's mouth. I was so relieved as we swam up past the whale's huge head. We hadn't been eaten!

Just then, the whale started to move. It was coming to the surface, and we were on top of it. As the whale's head came out of the water, we could see ocean for miles. That's when I noticed that the Magic School Bus was just a bus again. Just a bus sitting on top of a whale in the middle of the ocean.

Everyone was staring out the windows when Wanda asked, "What's that sound?"

I heard it, too. It was a low rumbling sound, and the bus started to shake. I saw a spout of water come up from below us, and the whole bus burst into the air.

"We're on the whale's blowhole!" Phoebe yelled.

"Yikes!" I yelled.

We were surrounded by a rush of water vapor as we rose higher and higher. Through the wet blur, I could see that the bus was sprouting wings.

The whole time, Janet stared out the window with her mouth opened wide. Then . . .

Whoa! We landed with a jolt. "We're in the parking lot of the science museum!" Janet exclaimed.

I couldn't believe my eyes. The Magic School Bus was back to normal — without jet wings *or* the Eat 'Em Up Cafe. There wasn't an ocean in sight — just a sea of school buses and the big science center building.

Janet blinked. "Wow," she said, shaking her head. "I never read about anything like *this* in my science book."

"Speaking of science books . . ." said Tim. "Look what I just found!"

He bent down and picked up two heavy books from the floor at the back of the bus.

"My book!" D.A. and Janet said at the same time.

We all got off the Magic School Bus — just in time to see Mr. O'Neatly's class *leaving* the science center. His students ran over to us. They were all talking at once.

"What happened?"

"You missed the whole tour!"

"It was amazing! We learned all about food chains!"

Then D.A. looked at them and smiled. "So did we," she said, holding up a piece of paper. "We *all* learned about food chains." She looked right at Janet and gave her a thumbs-up sign.

That was when we noticed that our

Incredible Edibles menus were gone. Instead, we were all holding paper handouts of the riddles — with all of our answers filled in!

"But . . . how did you kids answer all of the Incredible Edibles riddles? I didn't even hand those out until after we got to the museum," Mr. O'Neatly said.

Mr. O'Neatly looked curiously at Ms. Frizzle.

The Friz just smiled mysteriously and said, "You don't have to go to a museum to get a large helping of science, with a side order of food chain facts!"

"I think that's the Friz's way of saying we were nearly eaten alive about a zillion times!" Wanda whispered to Janet and me.

"At *my* school . . ." Janet began.

Uh-oh, I thought. I couldn't take any more bragging!

"At my school, we don't have anyone as *wild* or as *wonderful* as Ms. Frizzle," Janet finished.

All I could do was grin. "There's no doubt about it," I told her, "the Friz is one of a kind."

Join my class on all of our Magic School Bus adventures!

The Truth about Bats
The Search for the Missing Bones
The Wild Whale Watch
Space Explorers
Twister Trouble
The Giant Germ
The Great Shark Escape
The Penguin Puzzle
Dinosaur Detectives
Expedition Down Under
Insect Invaders
Amazing Magnetism
Polar Bear Patrol
Electric Storm
Voyage to the Volcano
Butterfly Battle